Ricky Ricotta's Mighty Robot

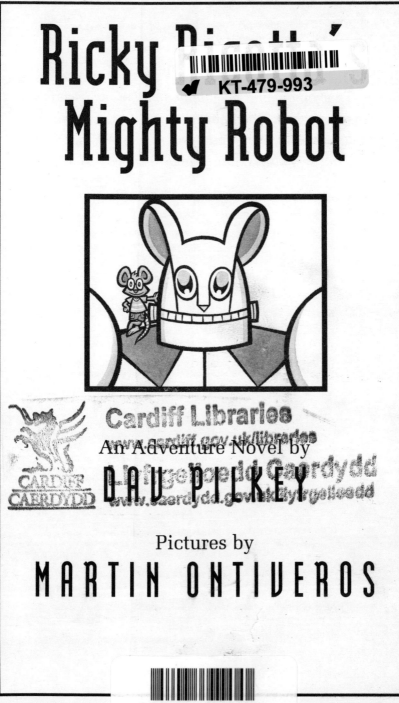

An Adventure Novel by

DAV PILKEY

Pictures by

MARTIN ONTIVEROS

For Walter Bain Wills — D. P.

To my mom and my family, to all of my friends everywhere (you know who you are), for their love and support, and most of all to Micki, and our two kitties, Bunny and Spanky — M. O.

Scholastic Children's Books
An imprint of Scholastic Ltd
Euston House, 24 Eversholt Street
London, NW1 1DB, UK
Registered office: Westfield Road, Southam, Warwickshire, CV47 0RA
SCHOLASTIC and associated logos are trademarks
and/or registered trademarks of Scholastic Inc.

First published in the US by Scholastic Inc, 2000
First published in the UK by Scholastic Ltd, 2001

This edition published in the UK by Scholastic Ltd, 2011

Text copyright © Dav Pilkey, 2000
Illustrations copyright © Martin Ontiveros, 2000

The right of Dav Pilkey and Martin Ontiveros to be identified as the
author and illustrator of this work respectively has been asserted by them.

ISBN 978 1 407107 58 5

A CIP catalogue record for this book is available from the British Library.

Printed in the UK by CPI Bookmarque, Croydon, Surrey.
Papers used by Scholastic Children's Books are made from wood
grown in sustainable forests.

1 3 5 7 9 10 8 6 4 2

This is a work of fiction. Names, characters, places, incidents and dialogues are
products of the author's imagination or are used fictitiously. Any resemblance to
actual people, living or dead, events of locales is entirely coincidental.

www.scholastic.co.uk/zone

Chapters

CHAPTER 1

Ricky

There once was a mouse
called Ricky Ricotta who
lived in Squeakyville with
his mother and father.

Ricky liked living with
his mother and father, but
sometimes he got lonely.

Ricky wished he had a friend
to keep him company.

"Don't worry," said Ricky's father.
"Some day something BIG will
happen, and you will find a friend."
So Ricky waited.

8

CHAPTER 2

The Bullies

Ricky liked school, but he
did not like walking to school.
This was because Ricky was
very small, and sometimes
bullies picked on him.

"Where do you think you are going?" asked one of the bullies.

Ricky did not answer. He turned and started to run.

The bullies chased him.

They knocked Ricky down
and threw his rucksack into
a dustbin.

KEEP OUR CITY
"SQUEAKY
CLEAN"

Every day, the bullies chased Ricky.
Every day, they knocked him down.
And every day, Ricky wished that
something BIG would happen.

CHAPTER 3
Dr Stinky McNasty

That day at school, Ricky
ate lunch by himself. Then
he went outside for playtime.

He watched the other mice
play a game of kickball.
Ricky did not know that
something BIG was about
to happen, but it was!

In a secret cave above
the city, a mad doctor was
planning something evil.

Dr Stinky McNasty had
created a mighty Robot.

"I will use this Robot to destroy the city," said Dr Stinky, "and soon, I will rule the world!"

Dr Stinky led his mighty Robot into town.

"Robot," said Dr Stinky, "I want you to jump and stomp and destroy this city!"

CHAPTER 4

The Mighty Robot

(IN

FLIP-O-RAMA™)

...O·RAMA

HERE'S HOW IT WORKS!

STEP 1
Place your left hand inside the dotted lines marked "LEFT HAND HERE". Hold the book open flat.

STEP 2
Grasp the right-hand page with your right thumb and index finger (inside the dotted lines marked "RIGHT THUMB HERE").

STEP 3
Now quickly flip the right-hand page back and forth until the picture appears to be animated.

(For extra fun, try adding your own sound effects!)

F L I P - O - R A M A 1

(pages 25 and 27)

Remember, flip only page 25.
While you are flipping, make sure
you can see the picture on page 25
and the one on page 27.
If you flip quickly, the two
pictures will start to look like
<u>one</u> animated picture.

Don't forget to add
your own sound effects!

LEFT HAND HERE

The Robot Jumped.

25

RIGHT
THUMB
HERE

The Kodak Jumped.

The Robot Jumped.

FLIP-O-RAMA 2

(pages 29 and 31)

Remember, flip only page 29.
While you are flipping, make sure
you can see the picture on page 29
and the one on page 31.
If you flip quickly, the two
pictures will start to look like
<u>one</u> animated picture.

Don't forget to add
your own sound effects!

LEFT HAND HERE

The Robot Stomped.

The Robot Stomped.

FLIP-O-RAMA 3

(pages 33 and 35)

Remember, flip only page 33.
While you are flipping, make sure
you can see the picture on page 33
and the one on page 35.
If you flip quickly, the two
pictures will start to look like
<u>one</u> animated picture.

Don't forget to add
your own sound effects!

LEFT HAND HERE

But the Robot Would Not Destroy the City.

RIGHT THUMB HERE

But the Robot Would
Not Destroy the City.

CHAPTER 5

Ricky to the Rescue

Dr Stinky was very angry.

"Destroy Squeakyville!" he cried. "Destroy Squeakyville!" But the Robot refused.

"I will teach you a lesson,"
said Dr Stinky. He pressed
a button on his remote control
and zapped the Robot with
a terrible shock.

Ricky was watching.

"Stop it!" Ricky cried. But Dr Stinky kept on zapping the Robot.

Finally, Ricky aimed a kickball at the evil doctor. Ricky kicked as hard as he could.

"BOING!"

The kickball bounced off Dr Stinky's head. Dr Stinky dropped the remote control, and it broke on the ground.

"Rats! Rats! RATS!" cried Dr
Stinky. "I shall return!" And he
disappeared down a manhole.

When the Robot saw what Ricky
had done, he walked over to Ricky.
Everyone screamed and ran.

But Ricky was not afraid. The Robot smiled and patted Ricky on the head.

Something BIG had happened after all!

CHAPTER 6
Ricky's Pet Robot

That afternoon, the Robot followed
Ricky home from school.

Soon they got to Ricky's
house. "Wait here, Robot," said
Ricky. Ricky went inside.

"Mum, Dad," said Ricky, "can I have a pet?"

"Well," said Ricky's father, "you've been a good mouse lately."

"Yes," said Ricky's mother, "I think a pet would be good for you."

"Hooray!" said Ricky.
"Uh-oh," said Ricky's parents.

CHAPTER 7

Ricky's Mighty Robot Helps Out

When Ricky's parents saw Ricky's new pet, they were not happy.

"That Robot is too big to be a pet," said Ricky's father.

"There is no room for him in our home," said Ricky's mum.

"But he is my friend,"
said Ricky, "and he will
help us around the house!"

Ricky's mighty Robot used
his super breath to blow all
the leaves out of their garden.
Ricky's dad liked that.

Ricky's Robot scared all the crows out of the vegetable patch. Ricky's mum liked that.

And when burglars drove
by the Ricottas' house,
they kept right on driving.
Everybody liked that!

"Well," said Ricky's father,
"I guess your Robot can live
in the garage."
"Hooray!" said Ricky.

CHAPTER 8

Back to School

The next day, Ricky and his Robot walked to school. The bullies were waiting for Ricky.

"Where do you think you're going?" asked one of the bullies.

"My Robot and I are going to school," said Ricky.

The bullies looked up and saw Ricky's mighty Robot. They were very frightened.

"Um...um...um...," said one
of the bullies, "can we carry
your rucksack for you, sir?"

"Sure," said Ricky.

The bullies helped Ricky get to
school safely.

"Is there anything else we can
do for you, sir?" asked the bullies.

"No, thank you," said Ricky.

CHAPTER 9

Show-and-Tell

That day at school, Ricky's class had show-and-tell. One mouse brought a baseball glove. Another mouse brought a teddy bear.

Ricky brought his mighty Robot.

Ricky's class got a free
ride on the Robot's back.

They flew up above the city
and over the mountains.

"This is fun!" said Ricky.

CHAPTER 10

Dr Stinky's Revenge

While Ricky's class was flying around in the sky, Dr Stinky sneaked over to the school. He wanted revenge!

Dr Stinky crept into Ricky's
classroom. He saw their pet lizard.

"This is just what I need!" said
Dr Stinky.

He took out a bottle of Hate
Potion No. 9 and put a drop
into the lizard's water dish.
The lizard drank the water.

Suddenly, the lizard began to grow and change. He got bigger and bigger. He got meaner and meaner.

Soon, the lizard turned into
an evil monster.

"Destroy Ricky and his Robot!"
said Dr Stinky.

"Yes, Master!" said the monster.

When Ricky's Robot saw the evil monster, he flew down to the school playground. Ricky and his class climbed off quickly. Then, the Robot turned towards the giant monster, and the battle began.

CHAPTER 11

The Big Battle

(IN FLIP-O-RAMA™)

FLIP-O-RAMA 4

(pages 73 and 75)

Remember, flip only page 73.
While you are flipping, make sure
you can see the picture on page 73
and the one on page 75.
If you flip quickly, the two
pictures will start to look like
<u>one</u> animated picture.

Don't forget to add
your own sound effects!

LEFT HAND HERE

The Monster
Attacked.

RIGHT
THUMB
HERE

The Monster
Attacked.

FLIP-O-RAMA 5

(pages 77 and 79)

Remember, flip only page 77.
While you are flipping, make sure
you can see the picture on page 77
and the one on page 79.
If you flip quickly, the two
pictures will start to look like
<u>one</u> animated picture.

Don't forget to add
your own sound effects!

LEFT HAND HERE

Ricky's Robot
Fought Back.

77

RIGHT
THUMB
HERE

Ricky's Robot
Fought Back.

FLIP-O-RAMA 6

(pages 81 and 83)

Remember, flip only page 81.
While you are flipping, make sure
you can see the picture on page 81
and the one on page 83.
If you flip quickly, the two
pictures will start to look like
<u>one</u> animated picture.

Don't forget to add
your own sound effects!

LEFT HAND HERE

The Monster
Battled Hard.

81

RIGHT
THUMB
HERE

The Monster
Battled Hard.

FLIP-O-RAMA 7

(pages 85 and 87)

Remember, flip only page 85.
While you are flipping, make sure
you can see the picture on page 85
and the one on page 87.
If you flip quickly, the two
pictures will start to look like
<u>one</u> animated picture.

Don't forget to add
your own sound effects!

LEFT HAND HERE

Ricky's Robot
Battled Harder.

RIGHT
THUMB
HERE

Ricky's Robot
Battled Harder.

FLIP-O-RAMA 8

(pages 89 and 91)

Remember, flip only page 89.
While you are flipping, make sure
you can see the picture on page 89
and the one on page 91.
If you flip quickly, the two
pictures will start to look like
<u>one</u> animated picture.

Don't forget to add
your own sound effects!

LEFT HAND HERE

Ricky's Robot
Saved the Day.

RIGHT
THUMB
HERE

Ricky's Robot
Saved the Day.

CHAPTER 12

The Electro-Rocket

The monster was defeated, and all of his evil powers went away. Soon, he turned back into a tiny lizard and never bothered anybody again.

"Rats! Rats! RATS!" cried Dr Stinky. "I will destroy that Robot myself!" He took his Electro-Rocket and aimed it at Ricky's Robot.

"NO!" screamed Ricky. He
leaped on to Dr Stinky just as
the evil doctor fired his rocket.

Up, up, up went the rocket.
Ricky's Robot flew after it.
But he was not fast enough.

The rocket came down
and exploded.

"Ka-BOOM!" Right on
Dr Stinky's secret cave.

CHAPTER 13

Justice Prevails

"Rats! Rats! RATS!" cried Dr Stinky.
"This has been a bad day for me!"

"It is about to get worse,"
said Ricky.

Ricky's mighty Robot picked
up Dr Stinky and put him
in the city prison.

CHAPTER 14

Back Home

That night, the Ricotta family
had a barbecue in the back garden.
Ricky told his mum and dad all
about their adventures that day.

"Thank you for saving the city,"
said Ricky's father.
"And thank you for saving each other," said Ricky's mother.

"No problem," said Ricky ...

"that's what friends are for."

HOW TO DRAW
RICKY'S ROBOT

107

HOW TO DRAW THE MONSTER

1.

2.

3.

4.

5.

6.

About the Author and Illustrator

DAV PILKEY created his first stories as comic books while he was in elementary school. In 1997, he wrote and illustrated his first adventure novel for children, The Adventures of Captain Underpants, which received rave reviews and was an instant best-seller – as were the other books that followed in the series. Dav is also the creator of numerous award-winning picture books. He and his dog live in Seattle, Washington.

It was a stroke of luck when Dav discovered the work of artist MARTIN ONTIVEROS. Dav knew that Martin was just the right illustrator for the Ricky Ricotta's Mighty Robot series. Martin lives in Portland, Oregon. He has a lot of toys as well as two cats, Bunny and Spanky.

Visit Dav Pilkey's Extra-Crunchy
Web Site O'Fun at:
www.pilkey.com

COMING SOON:

Ricky Ricotta's Mighty Robot
vs

The Mutant Mosquitoes from Mercury

The Voodoo Vultures from Venus

The Mecha-Monkeys from Mars

The Jurassic Jack Rabbits from Jupiter

The Stupid Stinkbugs from Saturn

The Uranium Unicorns from Uranus

The Naughty Night Crawlers from

Neptune

The Un-Pleasant Penguins from Pluto